THUNDERBIRDS

DESPERATE INTRUDER

BY AISLING O'HAGAN

BOXTREE

DESPERATE INTRUDER

Brains and Tin-Tin were almost ready to set off on their long-planned trip. As a well-earned break from their work on Tracy Island, they were travelling to Lake Anasta, in the Sahara Desert, to look for a submerged temple and its priceless buried treasure.

' Do you really think you'll find that long-lost treasure, Brains?' asked Scott.

'Oh er, I sure hope so,' replied Brains. 'It seems 90 per cent certain there's something at the bottom of that lake.'

'We're meeting up with Professor Blakey from the museum,' said Tin-Tin. 'We've heard he's the best man in his field.'

'Well, I'm sure you two know what you're doing,' said Mr Tracy. ' But don't forget, stay in touch at all times. You'd better get started, Virgil's ready to launch Thunderbird 2'

After a few hours' journey, Virgil touched down in the vast expanse of desert and unloaded the trailers and equipment. Then Brains and Tin-Tin set off to meet Professor Blakey in their jeep.

DESPERATE INTRUDER

'Brains, old boy,' said the Professor, pulling up at the rendezvous in a battered taxi. 'Jolly good to see you. Now, I suggest a quick trip down to the lake for a jolly good recce.'

'O-OK, Professor,' said Brains, thrilled at the thought. 'But how about a c-cool drink in the trailer before we go. Then you can tell us all about the temple.'

'Splendid idea,' agreed the Professor. 'Splendid.'

As the three explorers excitedly talked through their plans, little did they realise that their tranquil location wasn't quite as deserted as it seemed.

At that very moment they were being watched by none other than an evil criminal mastermind, the Hood. Eager to get his own greedy hands on the Anasta treasure, he had installed himself in a submarine and was patrolling the lake.

'The treasure that International Rescue seeks will be mine,' hissed the villain. 'Then I will see that my enemies stay at the bottom of Lake Anasta. Ha ha ha!'

DESPERATE INTRUDER

Later that afternoon, as the sweltering sun was setting, Brains and Tin-Tin decided it was time to explore the lake. Dressed in their diving gear and laden down with heavy equipment, they dived down to the bottom of the lake, and it wasn't long before Tin-Tin screamed with excitement, 'There it is, Brains. There's the temple!'

Like a scene from a fairytale, the sunken temple lay almost intact, with its grey stone walls shimmering in the dark waters. After surveying the inside, Brains took out his chisel and chipped off a small piece of stone from one of the huge columns. A tiny sample would be enough for Professor Blakey to confirm that this was where the treasure lay.

The explorers could hardly sleep for excitement that night as the results of the Professor's experiments had been even better than they expected. But no sooner had Brains called the Tracy Headquarters to relay the news than he was disturbed by a knock at his door.

'I g-guess Tin-Tin can't sleep either,' he thought as he got out of bed.

But, to his horror, it wasn't Tin-Tin. A dark, bearded stranger glared at him with threatening, yellow eyes.

'Who a-are you?' demanded Brains. 'W-What do you want?'

At International Rescue base the next morning, Scott was urgently called to his father's office. 'I don't get it, Scott,' said Mr Tracy. 'Brains hasn't checked in yet this morning. He's never been late before and I'm getting worried. I'll keep trying on the auto-transmitter, but I don't like it at all.'

Back by the shores of Lake Anasta, Jeff Tracy's calls echoed round the empty trailers. Outside, less than half a mile away, Brains was in the sweltering sun, buried up to his neck in the burning sand, while Tin-Tin and the Professor lay unconscious in their rooms.

'Tin-Tin...Pro...fessor, where are you?' whispered Brains, hardly able to speak. 'What happened?...That stranger...those staring eyes. If only I could get to my radio!'

'What would you do then my friend?' asked an eerie voice above him. 'Inform your friends at International Rescue? No, that is out of the question.'

As Brains looked up into the dazzling sun he could just make out the figure of the evil, bearded stranger.

DESPERATE INTRUDER

"Where are the others?' Brains whispered. 'W-What have you done with the others?'

'I shall deal with them later,' said the Hood. 'But first I want information. Where is the treasure concealed in the temple?'

'I don't know,' replied Brains. 'P-Please...give me some water!'

'Tell me where the gold is,' demanded the fiend, 'and I shall let you and your friends go. It is a simple choice to make.'

Back at headquarters, Scott Tracy burst into his father's office. 'Father, the emergency signal's gone off. That means...'

'Yes, I know,' interrupted Mr Tracy. 'That settles it, Scott. You'd better get out there fast and I'll send Virgil and Gordon on with Thunderbird 2.'

Within minutes, Scott was strapped into the pilot's seat in Thunderbird 1. The entire swimming pool in front of the Tracy villa slid slowly sideways to reveal a hidden underground launch pad. With a roar from its powerful engines, Thunderbird 1 soared into the sky, taking Scott swiftly towards the danger zone.

DESPERATE INTRUDER

Time was running out fast for the explorers. Back at the lake, Brains was becoming delirious. The Hood now sat behind the controls of his submarine, planning an evil scheme to outwit the Tracy brothers.

'In just 10 more minutes I shall go and see if my friend from International Rescue has changed his mind. No man can stay in the burning sun for long without having his tongue loosened.'

Then, laughing loudly, he swung his periscope round. His glee turned to fury when he saw Thunderbird 1 circling the area above.

'International Rescue!' hissed the villain. 'What is going on?'

Up in the sky, Scott radioed back to base. 'I've been flying over the danger zone for some time now, Father. The trailers are there but I can see no sign of Brains and the others...Wait! I can see Brains down below in the sand - he's buried up to his neck!'

Under the waters of Lake Anasta, through his periscope, the Hood watched Scott making a vertical landing at the side of the lake.

'So, they have found my victim in the sand,' he fumed. 'However, I

can turn this setback to my advantage. I now have the chance to destroy International Rescue utterly...after they lead me to the treasure.'

Meanwhile, Scott had landed and was at the side of Brains who was barely conscious.

'Scott, Scott,' whispered Brains. 'Thank heavens. Where's Tin-Tin...and the Professor?''

'We'll soon find them,' replied Scott as he tried to trickle some water into Brains' blistered mouth. 'Now let's get you out of here.'

While Scott dug deep into the hot sand to free his friend, Virgil landed Thunderbird 2 and went in search of the others. He found them inside the trailer and, minutes later, had managed to bring them round.

'Tin-Tin,' insisted Virgil. 'Try again. You said there was a stranger...'

'Yes,' replied Tin-Tin in a weak voice. 'With terrible eyes. I couldn't look away from him. It was horrible!'

DESPERATE INTRUDER

Once Professor Blakey had been safely escorted home by rescue helicopter, Scott radioed headquarters to tell his father the news. Then he relayed Jeff Tracy's stern orders to the others.

'Dad's relieved you're all safe. But he wants us all back at base in the morning. He says International Rescue is not set up to go joy-riding round on treasure trails.'

Later that night, as everyone lay sound asleep, Tin-Tin woke, startled, to find Brains, in diving gear, at the foot of her bed.

'What is it,Brains? What are you doing at this hour?' she whispered.

Brains explained to Tin-Tin that he couldn't sleep. He was sure that someone was spying on them and that the whole expedition had been used to draw International Rescue into a trap.

'There's only one place a spy could be observing us from,' said Brains. 'The centre of the lake. I've got to try and make amends for all the trouble I've caused.'

'But you're not going to the lake tonight!' cried Tin-Tin.

'Yes I am!' said Brains. 'I've got to see what's down there. I want you to keep in touch with me on talk-back.'

'All right,' said Tin-Tin, frowning. 'But I don't like it.'

As Brains swam under the surface of the dark lake he began to wonder if his theory was right. Then, as he reached the temple walls, his oxygen tank knocked away a stone, neatly placed to disguise a cable running along the floor of the lake. Little did he know, but at that moment Brains had woken the evil Hood, by activating an alarm in his submarine.

'So,' exclaimed the Hood. 'I have visitors. I shall go and meet them.'

As Brains was tracing the cable around the outside of the temple, he stopped suddenly as, to his horror, he came face-to-face with the evil villain who had tortured him. Unable to escape the power of the Hood's hypnotic eyes, he fell into a trance.

'Now I must find the treasure before his friends find him,' said Hood. And with that he pressed a detonater and an almighty explosion blew up the temple, scattering gold and jewels amongst the rubble.

DESPERATE INTRUDER

Hearing the blast, Tin-Tin immediately ran to wake the boys. 'I tried to stop him,' she cried. 'But he wouldn't listen. We've got to go down there and rescue him straight away!'

While Scott waited in the trailer with Tin-Tin, Virgil steered Thunderbird 2 to the side of the lake and released Thunderbird 4 from its pod into the water. Gordon lowered the mobile lighting rig and began to probe the murky depths of the lake.

'The temple is in ruins,' Gordon reported back to base. 'But I can see bubbles coming from underneath some rubble here. Scott, get down here with the aeroscopic lifting equipment. It might be Brains.'

Gordon never saw the Hood's ship creeping up behind him. Suddenly, violent explosions tore through the tail of his craft. Like a flash, Gordon swung his ship round and headed, full power, after his attacker. The Hood's craft was no match for Thunderbird 4. It fired two powerful missiles and blasted the enemy ship up towards the surface. Through the floating fuselage, Gordon saw the Hood open up his escape hatch and climb out.

With the enemy out of the way, Gordon raced back to the spot where

DESPERATE INTRUDER

Brains lay pinned beneath a large stone column, breathing the last of his precious oxygen. Minutes later Scott arrived, armed with a giant air balloon which he used to lift the stone. With only seconds to spare, Brains was wrenched out and brought to safety.

It took a couple of days, and plenty of Grandma's delicious meals, to restore Brains' and Tin-Tin's strength. Then, the first thing they did was to visit Professor Blakey, who was recuperating in hospital.

'We're so glad you're better, Professor,' said Tin-Tin. 'But now that the world has heard about our discoveries at Lake Anasta, how does it feel to be a celebrity?'

'Oh, not so bad,' replied the Professor. 'But, I say, how are you two fixed over the next couple of months? I've been reading about some old treasure sunk in the South Seas 400 years ago.'

Brains and Tin-Tin stared at each other in horror. They quickly gathered their things and made towards the door.

'Er, visiting time is over now,' said Tin-Tin. 'We really must be off...So long, Professor...must dash!'

First published in the UK 1992 by BOXTREE LIMITED,
36 Tavistock Street, London WC2E 7PB

3 5 7 9 10 8 6 4 2

Copyright (c) 1992 ITC Entertainment Group Ltd.
Licensed by Copyright Promotions Ltd.

Design by Root Associates Ltd.

1-85283-717-9

Printed in Great Britain by Butler & Tanner Ltd.

A catalogue record for this book is available from the British Library.